FLIP FLOP BOP

by Matt Novak

A NEAL PORTER BOOK
ROARING BROOK PRESS
BROOKFIELD, CONNECTICUT

To Tabitha and Sophia,
my flip floppin' girls

Copyright © 2005 by Matt Novak
A Neal Porter Book
Published by Roaring Brook Press
Roaring Brook Press is a division of Holtzbrinck Publishing Holdings Limited Partnership
2 Old New Milford Road, Brookfield, Connecticut 06804

Distributed in Canada by H. B. Fenn and Company Ltd.

Library of Congress Cataloging-in-Publication Data
Novak, Matt.
Flip flop bop / Matt Novak. —1st ed.
p. cm.
"A Neal Porter book."
Summary: Presents an easy-to-read, rhyming celebration of summertime's favorite footwear—flip flops.
ISBN 1-59643-049-4   [1. Thongs (Sandals)—Fiction.   2. Shoes—Fiction.   3. Stories in rhyme.]   I. Title.
PZ8.3.N8555Fl 2005   [E]—dc22   2004017639

Roaring Brook Press books are available for special promotions and premiums.
For details contact: Director of Special Markets, Holtzbrinck Publishers.

First edition 2005
Printed in China
2 4 6 8 10 9 7 5 3 1

CLIPPETY CLOP

CLIPPETY CLOP

Skipping

Hopping

Drippety Drippety
Drop
Drop
Drop

Flippety Flippety
Flop
Flop
Flop

Bubbles and Flippers

Buttons and Zippers

Now it's time for Bunny Slippers

Hippity Hop Hippity Hop

Flippety Flippety

Flop

Flop

Flop